KATE'S GIANTS

Valiska Gregory

illustrated by **Virginia Austin**

WALKER BOOKS

AND SUBSIDIARIES

LONDON · BOSTON · SYDNEY

In Kate's new room there was a door,
small and curious as Kate herself.
"It's the door to the attic," said her parents.

But Kate didn't like it.
"What if scary things come through
that door?" she said.

And sure enough,
when Kate was tucked in tight,

and shadows moved like fingers on the wall,
she thought they did.

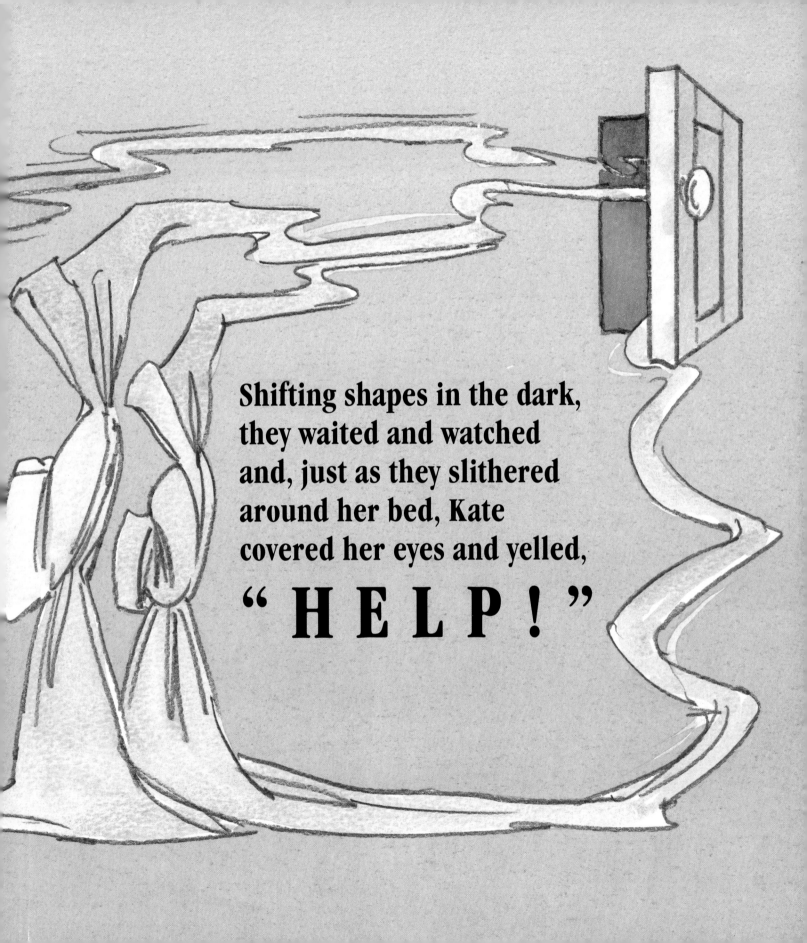

Shifting shapes in the dark, they waited and watched and, just as they slithered around her bed, Kate covered her eyes and yelled, "**HELP!**"

Her father said, "If you can think them up,
then you can think them out."
"It won't be easy," said Kate.

She saw a tree move its witchy hand.
"What if animals come through
that door?" she said.

And sure enough, when Kate was all alone,

she thought she heard a scritching sound –

a lion with teeth as sharp
as claws, two hungry bears
with lumbering paws.
They growled and they
roared so loud, that she
could barely call out,

"HELP!"

Her mother said, "If you can think them up,
then you can think them out.
Just take a deep breath before you think."

Kate heard thunder rumbling the panes.
"But what if giants come through
that door?" she said.

And sure enough, as Kate sat in the dark,

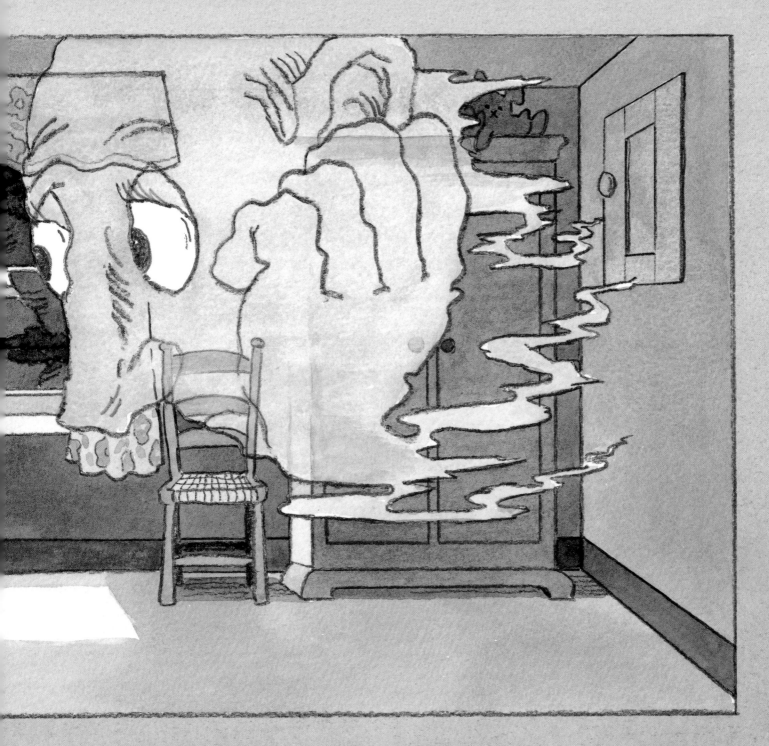

she thought she saw them come.

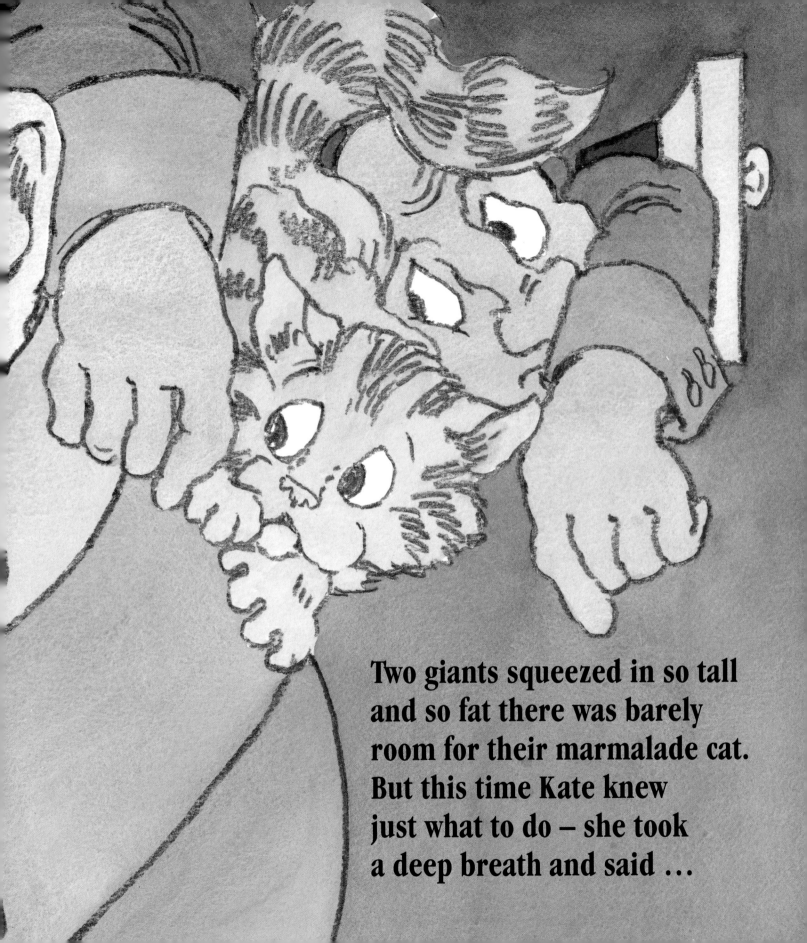

Two giants squeezed in so tall and so fat there was barely room for their marmalade cat. But this time Kate knew just what to do – she took a deep breath and said …

"STOP! If I can think you up,

then I can think you out.”

And sure enough, she did.

Outside the window,
the moon was round
as an owl's eye.

Kate thought about the attic door.
"I wonder if friendly things could come through
that door," she said.

And sure enough, she thought they did.

Kate smiled a friendly giant smile.
"This is the best part," she said…

"If I can think them out,
then sometimes, I can think them in!"